Summer Reading

Summer Reading

Kate Sutherland

Thistledown Press Ltd.

Canadian Cataloguing in Publication Data

Sutherland, Kate, 1966 -
Summer reading
(New leaf series)
ISBN 1-895449-49-9
1. Women - Fiction. I. Title. II. Series.

PS8587.U74S8 1995   C813'.54   C95-920156-4
PR9199.3.S87S8 1995

Book design by A.M. Forrie
Cover art by Lia Sunshine Weingeist Harned
Set in Garamond
by Thistledown Press

Printed and bound in Canada
by Kromar Printing
Winnipeg, Manitoba

Thistledown Press Ltd.
633 Main Street
Saskatoon, Saskatchewan
S7H 0J8

Acknowledgements
"Jigsaw" and "Duck Hunting" have previously appeared in *Grain*, volume 20,
number 2, and volume 21, number 3, respectively.

The author would like to thank Lorna Crozier, Gerald Lynch, Ven Begamudré
and Paddy O'Rourke for their advice and encouragement at various points
in the evolution of these stories.

Passages quoted in "Summer Reading" are taken from *Wuthering Heights*
by Emily Brontë.
Lyrics quoted in "A World of Blue" are taken from "The Blue Skirt Waltz" by
Mitchell Parish and Vaclav Blaha.

This book has been published with the assistance of The Canada Council
and the Saskatchewan Arts Board.

Contents

Piecing a Quilt   9

Duck Hunting   16

me & men & whisky   23

Summer Reading   29

Jigsaw   39

Open Spaces   46

A World of Blue   50

Ghostwriting   56

Moving Away   60

For Katrysha

Piecing a Quilt

Phoebe's standing in the produce section of the Safeway when she notices him staring at her over his cart. She's trying to decide between broccoli and cauliflower though she doesn't much like either. She finds herself minding her mother's admonitions now that she's moved away from home. Dinner has to include a vegetable.

If Suzanne had been there she would've jangled her car keys and suggested a cheeseburger. But Phoebe hasn't seen Suzanne for months, not even before she moved.

He looks familiar, but that doesn't mean anything. She hasn't lived here long and people usually look familiar because they remind her of someone else.

He catches up with her at the cash register. As soon as she looks back at him, he takes the chance to speak. "Hey, I've seen you before, at a club downtown. Canadian Spaces, maybe. Do you like local music?"

"I just moved to town. I don't really know the bands yet."

"Welcome," he says. "I'm Daniel." He puts his hand out to shake hers.

"Phoebe," she replies. His hands are large enough to cover hers but his fingers are piano-player delicate.

As he walks away, she notes his sloping shoulders, his large feet. She wonders how he can be so awkward yet charming at the same time.

Friday night Phoebe's at a party. She stands with two girls from work. Her black sleeveless turtleneck is stark next to their colourful sundresses. She wishes she wasn't with them but she wouldn't have been brave enough to come alone. They're drinking vodka and 7-Up, Phoebe faster than the others.

Soon she's at the centre of a group of strangers, talking loudly and waving her arms around till her drink sloshes over the sides of the glass. Her friends from work are watching, tight-lipped, from their corner. Phoebe's felt that look on her own face before.

A bush party in grade eleven. Suzanne was showing off, jumping back and forth over a fire someone had built. Phoebe laughed with everyone else till Suzanne started complaining about the heat and stripping her clothes off piece by piece. She left when Suzanne was down to blue jeans and a black lace bra. Then she lay awake all night worrying about what might have happened to her.

Phoebe sees Daniel through the haze of smoke and vodka, leaning against the doorway watching her. He must've come in the back way and just stood there, she doesn't know for how long. He takes her glass out of her hand and puts it down near the sink.

"I'll drive you home," he says.

Instead, they go to his place for another drink. He lives in a rambling old house not far from her apartment building. The front steps are warped and creaking. She skips over the middle one; it doesn't look as if it could hold her.

An orange and black cat darts out when he opens the door. "I call her the Empress," he says. "She's not too friendly with strangers."

"Will she stay out all night?" Phoebe asks as he shuts the door behind them.

"Nah, she can get back in through the window."

He leads her upstairs to his bedroom right away. There's nothing in it but a mattress, some milk-crate bookshelves and a single lamp. The harshness of the bulb is lessened by a red T-shirt he's draped over it. Its rosy glow warms the room despite the emptiness. That and the crazy quilt spread over the mattress. He tells her his grandmother made it for him.

She likes the room better than her own. Her small bed, so small her feet stick out over the end. And the pale blue comforter she brought from home. She wonders why she never thought of bringing one of her mother's quilts. The one she helped her mother make the summer before high school, she could've brought that one.

She sits next to Daniel on the edge of the mattress and he toys with the fringe of her buckskin jacket. She's drinking the beer he gave her, quickly, in small sips. What would her mother think, her sitting there next to a man she just met? She knows what Suzanne would think.

"I've never made love before," she blurts. She can almost hear Suzanne's laugh as she speaks. But she's lost her nerve now, she's starting to sober up.

"It's okay," he says. "We don't have to."

She wakes next to him just before daylight. They're under the quilt, still dressed. She wants to reach over and touch him, rub her fingers against the stubble of his beard. Make this real. But she doesn't want him to see her in daylight, pale and mascara-smudged. The vodka pounds in her head as she pulls herself erect. She scrambles on the floor for her jacket and shoes and tiptoes down the stairs, through the porch, past the cat's unblinking eyes.

He sends letters from those few blocks away. She's charmed when she finds the first thin envelope in her mail box. The next is more elaborate. He encloses drawings, mostly of the Empress. She calls the number he's inked at the bottom.

There's nearly always a crowd at his house, and she likes feeling part of it. They're all musicians and writers, at least they say they are. Mostly she just listens, stroking the cat in her lap.

Daniel doesn't say much to her when other people are around. Sooner or later though, they go upstairs and he reads poetry to her. He says he writes poetry but he never reads from his own. Usually he chooses e.e. cummings. They marvel over the way the words fit together, argue about what they mean.

Phoebe figures sex is the next step, and one night it happens. He sits beside her on the mattress and takes her hand. He kisses her shoulder, then her neck, but not her lips. It occurs to her that he never looks at her when he touches her but she pushes the thought away.

It hurts. She hears herself pleading with him to stop, in a voice louder than she expected. But he doesn't stop. He keeps pushing into her. She fills her mind with the people downstairs, if they can hear, what they're thinking.

When it's over she wants to laugh with him, make a joke of her inexperience. She wants him to reassure her it will be better next time, but he doesn't say anything. She's wet between her legs and she thinks it must be blood. She apologizes about the mess on his quilt. He tells her it's okay. He gets her a towel then crawls under the sheets and goes to sleep in silence.

In the morning she struggles to the bathroom to clean herself up. She flushes thick strings of blood down the toilet and stuffs a wad of Kleenex into the crotch of her underpants.

She'd like to call in sick, stay in bed with him all morning. Stay connected somehow. But he's facing away from her, and she's afraid he's only pretending to sleep.

She fingers the uneven bloodstain on the quilt. It's nearly lost in the pattern. All those reds and purples pieced together almost haphazardly. Nothing like her mother's careful work, Job's Tears or the Star of Bethlehem in pastel prints. Quilts she'd been afraid to sleep on.

Later, walking to work, she moves gingerly. She imagines the blood clotting and joining her legs together, trapping the space he's made inside her.

Two days pass and he doesn't phone. It's Thanksgiving weekend and she's alone and still bleeding. She thinks the flow is less now but she isn't sure. She's afraid she's hemorrhaging to death, she's heard of that. She wishes she could tell someone, so they'd know what had happened to her when they found her.

On the fourth day, when the blood is just a rosy swirl on her white cotton underpants, she calls him.

"Um, there's a band I want to see playing at Canadian Spaces," she says. "Do you want to go?"

"I can't," he says. "I have to, um, I mean . . ." Abruptly he tells her, "It's not right for me to see you. Your first should've been someone who loves you. I don't love you."

She knows he doesn't love her. She doesn't love him. But she didn't want to hear him say it. She'd been willing to pretend, to make it right that way.

Besides, she's not sure he's saying what he really thinks. She's afraid it was the ugliness, the blood. Her crying out in pain instead of pleasure. Always waiting too long, doing things the wrong way.

Phoebe goes home for a week at Christmas. She doesn't know she's going to call Suzanne until she finds herself dialing the number. She and Suzanne had shared their other firsts. First cigarette, first drink. But not sex.

Suzanne had had her first lover at fourteen and her 100th at eighteen. She'd reached the landmark figure just before graduation.

"100th time or 100th man?" Phoebe had asked.

"100th man," Suzanne had replied, tossing her head.

Phoebe had wondered if he knew, if he appreciated his significance.

She wasn't going to tell Suzanne her own story, sitting opposite her now in Smitty's coffee shop. Suzanne would mock her for having left it so long. She feels good sitting there though. Knowing she's been initiated into the sisterhood, taking pride in that.

She hadn't realized how much it mattered until now. By the middle of their senior year, the tension between them over Suzanne's sexual exploits had grown so great that they barely spoke. She'd detached herself from Suzanne, from everyone. Stopped going to the parties. At the end of it, she'd been glad to get a clerical job out of town.

Phoebe tries to see Suzanne from six months' distance. She's pale and distracted. She indecisively studies the menu, continually pushing strands of faded blonde hair out of her eyes.

Suzanne breaks the silence. "I'm pregnant," she says. "I'll have it in the spring." Her voice is so even that Phoebe doesn't know whether to congratulate her or say she's sorry.

"We're really happy . . ."

"Congratulations," Phoebe breaks in.

"Phil and me, we're getting married." She looks as if she's going to cry.

Phoebe waits.

"I'm scared," she says. "Not the childbirth, not that. But a stillbirth, or a deformed baby. I don't deserve a baby, Phoebe. I don't deserve to be happy. I've done everything wrong, you know that."

Phoebe doesn't know what to say. She reaches out to touch Suzanne's hand.

Phoebe decides to make a quilt for Suzanne's baby. On her lunch break she goes to a fabric store downtown.

She spends a long time in the store, breathing in the smell of fresh bolts of cloth, touching each one. She chooses a delicate floral pattern in two muted shades. The centre will be white with pinks and greens bordering it.

She steps into the harsh winter light, the package snug under her arm. A man is coming down the sidewalk, head bent, ploughing into the wind. Something about the way he walks reminds her of Daniel. She suddenly pictures him with his grandmother's quilt in the crook of his arm, taking it to the dry cleaners. She wonders if he did that, if he's removed all traces of her from his house.

She stands in the cold watching the man continue up the street, his shoulders hunched forward under a coat that's too big for him.

Phoebe pieces the quilt together carefully. The first part is the most difficult, cutting the unwieldy fabric into rectangles and strips. But she grows accustomed to the materials.

She lines up the edges of the pieces then sews them together with small, even stitches, making sure the corners don't pucker. With each strip she adds, the pattern becomes more clearly defined, her own pattern.

She likes the orderliness of it, each rectangle enclosed by a larger rectangle. It's not perfect, the corners don't always quite meet. But she likes this too. The mistakes prove she made it herself.

The baby is three weeks old when Phoebe arrives with her gift.

Suzanne beams. "We'll just set her on it for a minute, so she doesn't make a mess of it."

"She can mess it up. It's hers to use."

"It's the nicest thing anyone's given her, Phoebe. I know, why don't we take a picture?"

She sets the baby down and focuses the camera. Phoebe watches. The baby is a pink, wrinkled rose. She is the centre, the fabric from which the rest grows.

Duck Hunting

Tina stands in front of the school, scuffing the toe of one running shoe against a crack in the cement. The 3:30 bell rang a few minutes ago and the front lawn is nearly deserted. Only a huddle of girls left, sharing a cigarette. Tina thinks about joining them but she doesn't smoke and it's too cold to just sit there.

Her red monsoon jacket balloons out in the November wind, exaggerating the thinness of her legs below it. She draws her hands up into her sleeves and stands shivering. She should be wearing a ski jacket this time of year but her dad's never up in the morning to make her.

He's been working nights at the meat-packing plant ever since their hunting trip in September. He leaves before she's home from school and doesn't get back till long after she's asleep. His rotation on night shift has never gone on this long before. Tina figures he must have volunteered. It's like he's avoiding her.

She stares down the street toward their house for a minute, then whirls around and heads the other way. Downtown. She hates the empty house. When she was a kid she filled it with books. The reading habit stuck, which helps in school, but the books aren't enough anymore.

She walks right past the gas station where Mitch works. His boss's truck is parked outside so she can't go in. Mitch gets in trouble for having friends visit, his boss thinks they steal things. She turns down the alley and slips in the side door of the hotel.

"Hey, Tina," Johnny says from behind the bar, his speech a bit garbled. He has no teeth. He's got false ones, but he hardly ever wears them, leaves them sitting up on the bar instead. Nobody minds. Same as nobody minds a fourteen-year-old hanging around after school.

Johnny pretends he lost his teeth in a fight but Tina knows he just spent too many years in this town without a dentist. He told her so once. She's the kind of person people tell things to.

"The usual?" he asks, already pouring her a Coke. He always gives her a free Coke. Says he worries about her: "I know what happens to you kids on the street without enough money." Tina has money, her dad leaves a few bills on the kitchen counter every morning. But she takes the Coke anyway, she likes to feel someone's looking out for her.

She's not thinking about this today though. She's thinking about her mother, something she never used to do. Not before the hunting trip anyway. The girls at school find that hard to believe. Especially Sherri MacIsaac who's adopted and talks on and on about finding her real mother.

Tina's always felt like having someone else who would take her dad away altogether. It's true that when he does notice her he treats her like a boy, at least he used to, but she never really minded that. She likes baseball and cars. Even fishing, though she doesn't much like baiting the hook. But hunting.

"Johnny, did you know my mother?"

"Sure, Tina. A real bright light your ma . . . " And his voice goes all soft.

The bright part sounds right. Tina remembers sparkling eyelids and bright lips leaning over her bed. But she's surprised at the tone of his voice. She expected him to be on her dad's side. Her dad drank at the hotel a lot when her mother first left.

"Why d'you think she took off?"

"I don't know. Just had to get out I guess — not enough in this town for a woman like her. Wasn't meant to be anybody's wife, or anybody's mother." He shrugs.

Tina sits quiet after that till Johnny says she should go. "Happy hour crowd's coming in. This is no place for you at night." He's

been hustling her out at dinner time ever since work started up
at the construction site on the corner. He says it's not right the
way the men look at her, her just a kid still.

Across the street Mitch is getting ready to close the place and
he's glad to see her. She usually cashes out for him, she's quicker
at math. She figures his boss would be pretty surprised.

Soon they're clattering in the back door of his parents' house.
It's a tiny bungalow that's crammed full. Especially the front room
— gold shag carpet, an orange floral-patterned living room set
and knick-knacks cluttering every shelf. None of the spareness
of her own house.

"Hey, Flo!" Mitch calls out. "What's for dinner?"

"Can't you say mum like everybody else's kid?" Flo grumbles.
She seems tired. She's so small and thin that it always looks as if
her skin is stretched tight over the fine bones of her nose and
cheeks. Tonight her face sags somehow. But she smiles when she
sees Tina.

Tina has trouble smiling back. She knows what's for dinner.
The thick, oily smell of duck practically choked her the minute
they walked in. She feels like she felt standing in that field next
to her dad.

She'd kind of expected the gun to knock her flat, like in the
movies. But it just jolted her a little and somehow she managed
to hit a duck. She didn't kill it though.

It came down still fluttering one wing in a crazy panic. She
didn't see where it landed but she thought she could still hear
that one wing thudding against the ground, even over the shot
ringing in her ears. Then she realized it was her pulse. She
doubled over and puked right there in the dry yellow grass.

Her dad didn't say anything after that. Just walked over to
where the duck was and snapped its neck. He left it lying there
and told Tina to get into the truck.

When they got home he poured himself a rye and Coke and
sat at the kitchen table for hours, mumbling about her mother
and her and women, tracing the wet circle from his glass on the

arborite surface, over and over. Her mother's name, Sylvie. He loves her. He hates her. She's a bitch, a whore. And Tina, she'll be the same. She'll leave too. She's got breasts for christsakes. The kid's got breasts.

Tina shut herself in her room. She didn't want him to notice that — he ought not to. She held her knees close to her chest and rocked slowly back and forth.

"Hope you're hungry Tina," Flo says. "The old man got a duck. Sober enough to go hunting for a change, sober when he started anyway."

Flo and Mitch call him the old man, Tina doesn't even know what his first name is. She doesn't call him anything. He isn't usually around so she doesn't have to. But tonight he's hanging around the kitchen gloating about his duck and making faces at Flo behind her back.

The smell of the duck is making Tina queasy so she thinks up an excuse. "I'm not really hungry, I just had a plate of fries at the hotel."

Flo doesn't buy it. "You eat like a bird, honey. Who's going to fatten you up if I don't. Just skin and bones." She shakes her head.

"She looks pretty good to me," the old man pipes up from his corner.

Tina crosses her arms over her chest.

"Best thing I seen around here in a long time." He looks pointedly at Flo.

Mitch takes a step toward him and he disappears down the hallway in a hurry.

"It's all right, honey," Flo says. "Soon he'll pass out for the night and we can have dinner in peace."

Tina balances on the edge of the tub watching Flo do her face before work. She waitresses nights at the hotel. "I'm an Avon lady's dream," she says, hauling her make-up bag out from under the sink. It's an old, white suitcase, round with a bright satin lining.

Tina's never seen so many bottles and tubes. She doesn't wear much make-up herself, just a little eye-liner.

Flo starts with a coat of Noxema then rinses it off with water, barely splashing a drop on the vanity. She pats her face gently with a towel. Tina notices the discolouration around her eye, greenish-brown fanning out to her right temple. Mitch told Tina this sometimes happened but it's the first time Flo's let her see.

"Him," Flo says, inclining her head toward the bedroom where her husband sleeps. "Someone has to tell you girls how it is," she continues. "Not that Mitch would lay a hand on you, but still . . . I wish someone'd told me a few things before I got married."

Flo turns back to the mirror, smoothes a dab of foundation over her face evenly, until it disappears into her bangs and under her chin.

"Don't tell Mitch, mind you, you know how he gets."

Tina knows. One time she and Flo had crouched behind the chesterfield for a quarter of an hour while Mitch chased the old man through the house with one of the shotguns from the rack in the basement. It probably wasn't loaded but you never know.

Tina's afraid Mitch will go to jail one day because of him. She asked him once why he didn't just move out and he said he was worried about what would happen to Flo if he left. Tina tried to imagine what it must've been like when Mitch was younger. He's still thin, his features almost girlish. But he's tall with a kind of sinewy strength that the old man can't match anymore.

Flo finishes her face with dramatic strokes of eye-shadow and red, red lipstick, then moves on to her hair. She combs it back in sleek, brown feathers, fixes it with hairspray. It almost looks wet when she's done.

She turns to Tina as if she's about to say something really important but stops. She puts out her hand and touches Tina's downy hair.

"You're so lucky to have that lovely blonde, honey. You should grow it long."

Then Mitch is banging on the door yelling. "Flo, where's my work gloves?"

"Probably where you left them." She shakes her head. "Men." But she unlocks the door and goes down the hallway to look for them.

When Mitch is out back swearing over his car and Flo's gone to work, Tina curls up in the big, green chair in the basement to do her homework. She spends a lot of time down there working. She used to go outside and hang over the hood of Mitch's car, watching him work. But he would never answer the questions she asked. He said she wouldn't catch on, that it was different from being school smart.

Sometimes Mitch stays inside with Tina and plays his electric guitar without plugging it into the amp. From across the room it's a funny rustling sound that makes her feel restless. If he plugged it in, the old man would be down in a second to make fun.

Mitch and his friends tease her for caring about her homework. None of them even finished school. She keeps on though; it seems important. Even Johnny keeps telling her she should stay in school. She kids him that pretty soon he'll be pinning her tests on the door of the cooler where he keeps the beer.

Mitch wants to play guitar in a band more than anything. But he's only seventeen and already the joints of his fingers are painfully stiff. Too many winter afternoons crouched over someone else's engine without gloves — most of the work's too fine for gloves. Then nights he's out back working on his own.

Tina wakes up, arms cramped awkwardly around her history text. She can feel the imprint of the chair's rough fabric on her right cheek. She heads upstairs, past the back door and up into the kitchen, to see what time it is, if Mitch is still outside.

The old man's standing at the window, nursing his hangover with another drink.

"He's still out there, wasting time on that piece of junk. Fool."

"Flo?" Tina asks. She knows Flo can't be home yet but she has to say something, put some words between them.

"It's just you and me, baby. Old woman's still at the bar, probably getting it off with some guy."

"Oh." Tina starts backing toward the door.

"Where you going? You gonna leave the old man alone too? Hey?" He lunges forward quicker than she thought he could and clamps a hand over one of her breasts.

She's stumbling backwards and too soon she's reached the stairs. She's falling down the few steps to the back door, arms flailing wildly. Finally she lands on the floor among the boots and the shoes.

The old man's standing above her still, his bathrobe flapping open, his belly sagging over the twisted waistband of his jockey shorts. She grasps the banister and pulls herself to her feet. Her eyes fix for a minute on the shotguns hanging downstairs. From where she stands she can see the dark outline of their barrels against the white stucco wall. The old man's eyes follow hers, then the two of them are locked in a stare.

She stands straighter, tightens her grip. "Don't touch me. Don't you dare touch me."

me & men & whisky

It's a strain waking up in a strange man's bed to the sound of church bells ringing. I didn't think I had any religion left, but the guilt sets in pretty quick with all that solemn clanging in the background.

I never mean for this to happen. It's the whisky — Irish, scotch, bourbon, doesn't matter which. The first few glasses are a warm bath, my face prickles pink, my legs tremble. A couple more and I'm floating in the smoke-blue air. I stop listening to the man I'm talking with and just watch his lips move, the way they curve round his words. I find myself tipping into his open mouth.

This goes directly against my sun sign. Aquarians aren't known as heavy drinkers. We're supposed to be social about it, just a few to keep the conversation flowing. If I were Pisces, it would be a different story. They like to experience the alcohol, that hazy feeling. I guess that's what it means to drink like a fish.

Without an astrological predisposition, booze isn't much of an excuse. Now love, that'd be different. Love can excuse anything. If we're fated to be together, who cares how soon it starts.

I roll over to look at him and he looks good. Thin, tightly muscled arms and legs, long legs, the kind that look great in jeans and boots on CMT videos. Oddly angled cheekbones, but I like a man with a flaw. Dark, curly hair, eyelashes to match. I could fall in love. But then he might not.

He opens his eyes. Blue. I like blue. "Morning, Gina," he says. He remembers me, this is a good sign. He props himself up on one elbow and kisses me. Then he stands all the way up and the sheet falls away. Long legs all right. He says he's going to shower then he'll make me breakfast, do I like scrambled eggs.

Yes, I could fall in love. But I fell into the scotch before I found out under what sign of the Zodiac he was born. I don't like to leave fate to chance, so I grab his jeans off the floor by the bed and rifle in the pockets for his driver's licence. October. Damn, another Libra.

According to Linda Goodman's *Love Signs*, the Aquarius woman and the Libra man aren't a bad match. Comparatively, that is. It's best to steer clear of Libra men altogether. You can't trust them, they vacillate. One minute they could be kissing you and offering you eggs, the next explaining the two of you are just friends. A Libran asked me to marry him once. A day later, while I was still thinking it over, he met someone else. Aquarians aren't all that decisive, but Librans make me that way — decisive about ending relationships.

I get dressed and bolt for the door. I want to be out of there before he's back shaking water at me out of that beautiful hair. I hesitate for a minute in the front hallway: there's the weekend paper, still neatly folded. I flip to Jeane Dixon, quick, just to double check. She's with Linda Goodman: "Don't make any hasty romantic moves; you'll regret it." I hear the shower shut off just as I click the door behind me.

Walking down the street, I start to think, what if that was Sunday's horoscope, not Saturday's. Was it going home with him that was hasty, or disappearing so quick. I didn't even leave anything behind, say a lipstick, or an earring, that I could go back for if I changed my mind.

I fish my monthly star scroll out of my shoulder bag, but it doesn't clarify anything. Not a word about haste. "Friends could help you establish a new understanding with someone important to your happiness," it says. I head to my friend Rosalie's restaurant, The Organic Café. It's the only place open so early on a Sunday. Not many of the clientele are battling hangovers this time of day. Besides me, that is. Rosalie can give me advice, and fruit juice.

"Hey, kid," Rosalie calls across the juice bar. "What are you doing up this early?" I pull up a wooden stool and she gets a closer look. "You haven't been home yet, have you?"

I shake my head, no.

She mixes up something to restore vitamin C and slides it over the counter. It's too yellow and too thick, but I drink it down. Rosalie knows what she's doing. She's a Taurean earth mother, through and through. "You've got a story to tell," she says. "Spill it."

I tell her about my cowboy and ask her if she thinks I should go back there. It's not too late to pretend I just slipped out for some muffins or something. Maybe it could still work out.

"Your men never work out," she says. "Have you ever thought about women?"

She's asked me this before. Not for herself. She says I'm cute but too flaky, not her type. I have thought about women; Aquarians are very open sexually. But so far I haven't met a woman I feel that way about. "I think I prefer men," I say. "Besides, most of the books don't account for the gender variable that way. I need guidance."

"There is a *Gay Love Signs*," she tells me. "I saw it in a shop in Provincetown last year. You work in a bookstore, order it."

I wonder what my boss would think. It could put a damper on my romantic prospects with him. Not that I necessarily have any. He's always getting annoyed at me, the way I mix up the Religion and New Age sections.

"Ah, forget it," she says. "I wouldn't wish you on any woman in your present state."

"So what do you think I should do?"

"Drink less, stop reading newspaper horoscopes and get your chart done by a real astrologer, if you're serious about it."

It sounds as if she's rehearsed this.

"And go home, you look like shit."

I figure Rosalie's right, I'm due for a change, so I show up on time for work Monday morning. My boss does a double take. I've

traded in my gypsy skirt for something tailored, and I'm using a
chiffon scarf to tie back my hair instead of draping it round my
neck in a cloud.

By Wednesday, he's asked me out for dinner. I think about it
seriously, it seems like the responsible choice. He's a solid
business man, not too old. But I can't really get my mind around
the idea of me with a Capricorn. They're supposed to have warm
hearts under all that cold ambition but I've never gotten that far
with one. Besides, I've got to learn to say no. I say no this time.

Wednesday night, the goody-two-shoes kick has gone so far
I even call my parents. It's kind of nice at first, then my mother
asks me if there's anyone special in my life yet. She thinks I'm a
spinster at 25. I'm relieved when she puts my dad on, he doesn't
care much about that stuff. But he wants to know if I've thought
about going back to school this September, I don't want to be a
clerk in a store all my life, do I.

With life this bleak, I can't resist sneaking a peek at the
Thursday morning paper, just to see if there's any hope. "Trust
your instincts when it comes to romance," it says. I'm not so sure
about my instincts, but at least it points to romance. And sure
enough, not much before closing, he walks in. He seems unre-
markable at first. Tall and thin. Dirty blonde hair cut short.
Wire-rimmed glasses and a bulky, grey wool sweater. He browses
in the Philosophy section for a while before I catch his eye and
then he's got this winsome bewildered expression that draws me
over there. His sweater is coming unraveled at his wrists. "Can I
help you with anything?" I ask. Anything at all. I mean, it's my
job, right. I'm stone cold sober and I want to fall into this man's
arms, so there must be something in it.

Soon enough we're in the pub next door. Then in my
apartment. I have a book he wants to borrow, he couldn't afford
to buy anything at the store. Simone de Beauvoir's *Letters to Sartre*.
I haven't read it yet, but some time I will. One of the world's great
romances. I figure this is a meeting of Aquarian minds. I'm already
thinking of him as the professor, to tell Rosalie.

My apartment is practically empty. Just throw rugs and cushions and one of those hanging wicker chairs. I always think I'm
going to go traveling so I don't collect much stuff. Except candle
holders, all different kinds. I have a weakness for those. And
books I mean to read. But I do have some nice crystal glasses —
my mother passed them on when she gave up saving them for
my wedding — and a bottle of Glenlivet. He seems like he's worth
good scotch.

I pour us each a whisky and he wants to touch my bare feet
when I slip off my leather sandals. Before I know it we're half
naked. He's got this beautiful scar on his shoulder, so I show him
mine, a thin white line that curves under my left breast. He's not
impressed. He's already shuffling through his wallet looking for a
condom. His mind might be Aquarian but he's pretty business-like
when it comes to sex. As quick and casual as a Sagittarian would
be. I can't cope with the contradiction, so I send him home before
it goes any further. He's not as bad a miscalculation as the guy
who wanted cola to mix with his Glenlivet, but somehow worse.

"This can't go on any longer," I whine to Rosalie on the phone.

"No, no longer than another year or two," she answers back.
She's losing patience with me, she can't take my love life seriously.

I call in sick to work and spend Friday in bed.

Saturday, I usually go to The Organic Café for lunch. Lettuce
and tomato on whole grain bread, hold the sprouts. But I don't
want to see Rosalie today. I hate not being taken seriously. There's
a poster up on a telephone pole, advertising a psychic fair in the
United Church basement, so I go there instead.

The only astrologer is a computer. For five dollars it spits out
your chart with a palm reading and a handwriting analysis thrown
in free. Somehow, I don't think this was what Rosalie was
suggesting last week. I figure I'll get my tarot cards read, at least
it's a real person doing that.

He's got black, chin-length hair, a goatee and eyes so grey
they're almost purple. Those eyes drag me across the room. He
strokes his beard with long, long fingers. I guess he's a Leo with

that kind of presence, or no, probably Scorpio, sex appeal running out the door. "It's a dollar a minute," he says. "Are you interested in romance, or a career?"

I choose romance. He gets me to shuffle the cards before he lays them out, then he holds my hand gently while he deciphers them. I think about him touching me other places with those long fingers.

"I see a tall, dark, mysterious stranger," he says. That lets out the professor. It could be my cowboy, but he wasn't so mysterious. Kind of an open book, even if the pages are apt to change day to day. Then it dawns on me this fortune teller could be describing himself.

I file through my mental notes on Scorpions. "Mysterious." Check. "Hypnotic eyes." Check. "Comes closer to knowing the answers to the mysteries of existence than any other sign." Man, I hope so. And Aquarians and Scorpions are usually drawn together by something out of the ordinary, say, psychic phenomenon. We're supposed to be a solid match, if a chaotic one. But Linda Goodman insists that harmony can be attained through astrological wisdom and I bet he's tapped into that.

It's perfect. I wouldn't even have to get out of bed in the morning for the paper. Just roll over and ask, honey, what kind of day is it going to be. Tarot readings over breakfast. No more Jeane Dixon, I'd banish her for this live-in fortune-teller. My future at his fingertips, those beautiful fingers.

He holds my hand a little tighter and winks. Then I get it, just a pick-up line, and the spell of those eyes is broken. He probably doesn't have an ounce of psychic ability, Scorpio or no. I can't be taken in again. I tell him I've run out of money, so he'd better stop. He does, but says maybe he could give me a free consultation if we went for a drink later.

I'm thinking if I wrote my life story, some reviewer would say, "too many men, not enough plot." All of a sudden, I want real direction in my life. I want to figure out myself what happens next.

Summer Reading

From the dock, it looks as if the boat has drifted into the middle of the lake empty. Emma had rowed it out there and put down the anchor. Now she's scrunched down in the bottom, lying on the plastic cushions she took from the old lounger. She's reading *Wuthering Heights*.

The boat rocks in the wind. Nothing like the wild wind howling round the moors in the book, but it helps her get there. The cries of ducks and loons don't rouse her. She has forgotten the fishing rod she brought with her, though it jabs awkwardly into her leg, leaving an angry red mark.

Suddenly the boat rocks violently, banging Emma's head hard against the aluminum seat behind her. She comes up out of the book just in time to catch the tail end of Tory's laughter as she skis by too close. She sees then they're doing it on purpose, Steve at the wheel of the boat and Tory out behind. They circle round her again, closer still. The boat tugs at its anchor, drawn into Tory's wake. Soon they tire of the game and Emma is left alone again. Probably Steve has to get to his lifeguard job at the public beach.

When Emma's parents proposed she spend the rest of the summer at the lake with her aunt and uncle and Tory, it seemed an unexpected treat. Emma's dad was reluctant, but there was nothing else to be done. His mother was very ill and they had to fly to England. Even her grandmother's illness didn't take the shine off the lake for Emma. She barely knows her.

Emma had spent a few evenings with Tory before in the city, in her attic room, while their mothers laughed in the kitchen and their fathers made awkward conversation in the den. Tory always did her up with Aunt June's Avon samples, very cherry lipstick, passion pearl nail polish, while Emma read out loud from magazines. Emma would forget the wet polish on her toes and work them into the blue shag carpet as she read. Love stories from *True Romance*, horoscopes and numerology from the back pages of *Mademoiselle*, and the quizzes in *Cosmospolitan*. "What Kind of Friend Are You?" with results that spanned from "Doormat" to "Selfish B-i-t-c-h". Tory and Emma both fell safely in the middle, though it was hard to say, so many of the questions had to do with things that hadn't happened yet.

Emma had no magazines to bring with her to the lake. Her mom doesn't care about fashion. Even at the lake Aunt June wears delicate high-heeled sandals while Emma's mom's street shoes are as solid and boxy as the ones she wears to work with her nurse's uniform. They're sisters but they're not much alike. Their two fathers have even less in common. Next to Emma's thin, fair, spectacled father, her uncle is a dark bulldog of a man. Emma has seen the sour look on her dad's face when her mom suggests if he can't fix the leak in the downstairs toilet, perhaps her uncle can. And she has heard her uncle grumbling about how her dad, the professor, thinks he's better than everyone else, him and his books.

Emma packed some of her dad's books to take with her. Three thin paperbacks: *Wuthering Heights*, *Lolita*, and *The Scarlet Letter*. These titles were on the list her dad made up for her. He does this every year: summer reading. She wasn't sure if she'd have time to read them at the lake.

She and Tory have never had this much time together. Not since they were little girls and their families took a camping trip together. She remembers the two of them in shiny yellow rain slickers fishing off the dock. Emma was the one who caught a fish, a small perch that glittered silver and orange and white as she yanked it out of the water. But Tory had to take it off the hook, Emma couldn't bear its wild thrashing.

Tory is one for action, not for books. She doesn't have a library card, and she's never envied Emma's weekly trip to the library with her dad. But Emma tried to interest her in *Wuthering Heights* when she arrived at the cabin. She told Tory it's a love story like the ones in *True Romance* magazine, except longer. She tried to bring the book alive for Tory. Willful Cathy. Dark, wild Heathcliff. Linton, pale and blond and aristocratic. And Cathy's brother Hindley who hates Heathcliff and approves of Linton. How Cathy loves Heathcliff but marries Linton. Then Linton's sister Isabella falls for Heathcliff.

Tory quickly lost the thread and interrupted. "It sounds like "The Young and the Restless"," she said. "Except it takes a lot longer to get to the good parts. Besides, I'd rather have my own romance than read about someone else's."

She took Emma to meet Steve at his family's cabin a few doors down. To show him off. Her new boyfriend, she said, once they were beyond her parents' earshot.

Steve is blonde and athletic. The sort of boy all the girls at Emma's school fall for, except that he's into religion. This last part doesn't seem to bother Tory; she plays to it. She's begun to wear a lot of white and she asked Emma to call her Victoria, not Tory, in front of him. His brother Brian is a perfect opposite. His dark hair is long and tangled, his eyes a stormy blue. Beard stubble roughens his chin. Steve whispered to Tory that Brian had been in reform school, but didn't say what for. Tory wanted to speculate with Emma about this afterwards. But Emma could think only of his strong brown hands. "Heathcliff," she breathed to herself later in her bunk.

There were more days at Steve's cabin, or out in his boat. Emma began to feel like a tag-along-kid-sister, not a friend, though Tory's just fourteen herself, only one year older. "Look what the kids are wearing these days," she'd remark to Steve, eyeing Emma's black T-shirt and cutoffs. Then she'd spin round,

flouncing the skirt of her cotton sundress. Emma has a few
flowered dresses in the duffel bag she packed for the lake, but
she prefers the T-shirt and shorts. Tight, and clinging to the curves
that are just beginning. The first day she met him, Brian had
looked her up and down and nodded approvingly. "Basic black,"
he said, tugging at the black motorcycle jacket he wore every day,
no matter how hot.

Emma still sticks with Tory and Steve whenever she can. It
gives her an excuse to refuse her uncle's invitations to go fishing
or play cards. She's not sure why she's avoiding him. The first
day she'd watched a long time while he split birch for firewood.
There was something almost cruel in his face as the axe bit into
the wood. There was the sheen of sweat on his short, muscled
arms, the man-smell of him.

And with Tory and Steve she sometimes gets a glimpse of
Brian. Even at a distance, the sight of him gives her that feeling.
The same warm shiver she felt reading about the world's greatest
lovers, in a classmate's copy of *The Book of Lists* in the cloakroom
at school. But she thinks Brian barely notices her beside Tory,
her marmalade-coloured hair washed out by Tory's black curls.
Tory and Steve are mean about him when they're not teasing
Emma or sneering about the girls who wear crocheted bikinis on
the public beach. Whispering "jailbird" just loud enough for him
to hear. But still, there's a flash in Tory's eyes when Brian is around
that makes Emma nervous.

> *Even Heathcliff kept his hold on Cathy's affections unal-*
> *terably; and young Linton, with all his superiority, found*
> *it difficult to make an equally deep impression.*

Emma resolves to forget their trying to knock her out of the
rowboat and tell Tory how she feels. She doesn't want to reveal
this secret, raw and sensitive as her pale pink nipples, but she
feels she must. One of the questions in the *Cosmopolitan* quiz
asked: "Would you date a man your friend likes?" Tory hadn't
hesitated in answering "no."

The springs of the bunk-bed squeak as Emma leans down. "What do you think of Brian? Really?"

Tory shrugs.

"I kind of like him."

Tory hoots. "Give it up. He's practically a man, he'd eat a kid like you for breakfast."

> *"Nelly, help me to convince Isabella of her madness. Tell her what Heathcliff is: an unreclaimed creature, without refinement, without cultivation: an arid wilderness of furze and whinstone. I'd as soon put that little canary into the park on a winter's day, as recommend you to bestow your heart on him!"*

Emma holds her hurt to her like the book pressed tightly to her chest. She wonders where Tory disappears to when Steve lifeguards, the days she isn't on the beach with him. Then, in a half-sleep she thinks she hears Brian's voice under the window, calling out to Tory, sees Tory's bed is empty beneath her, a white blank in the darkness. In the morning, she can't be sure.

Emma stops talking to Tory, but Tory doesn't seem to notice.

A few days later, rummaging for a fishing rod in the shed behind the cabin, Emma is startled by Brian's velvet voice.

"Hey. What're you looking for?"

He's sitting on an old picnic table at the back of the shed, rolling a cigarette.

Emma just looks at him, her hands dangling uselessly. For a minute she thinks he's waiting for Tory here, a secret tryst. She feels sick.

But he's looking at her with interest. "C'mere."

She stops a little ways in front of him and he slides his cigarette into his shirt pocket and pulls her in the rest of the way. He kisses her hard and touches her small breasts gently through her thin, black T-shirt. Her puffy nipples harden to a smooth roundness under his fingers. Then he's gone, forgetting his pouch of Drum tobacco on the table.

*There was another rapid glance at the house, and
supposing himself unseen, the scoundrel had the impu-
dence to embrace her.*

Emma leaves the fishing rod and searches out a small clearing
in the bush behind the cabin where she won't be disturbed. She
sits cross-legged, book in her lap, warm with the shame and the
pleasure of what just happened. Tory and Steve have only kissed.
Tory said he wouldn't respect a girl who'd go any further.

The next time Emma sees Brian, he's on the gravelly beach in
front of the cabin with Tory and Steve. She almost loses her nerve
and walks right past till she hears Brian shouting after her: "Hey
look at her, walking along like a princess."

She always walks like that, straight-backed, from ballet lessons.
She grew up on *Ballet Shoes* and *A Little Princess*. She approaches
slowly.

"Yeah, a princess, pure as the driven snow," he adds, giving
an exaggerated wink.

Emma wishes she didn't blush so easily. But it feels good till
Steve chimes in with his mocking laugh. Then she wonders if
they all know, if it was some kind of joke. A bet. But Tory's staring
out past the reeds, over the water, not even listening.

"Not like you, you old tart," Brian turns to Tory. Steve
scrambles toward him making a fist. Tory doesn't respond.

*"She abandoned them under a delusion," Heathcliff
answered, "picturing in me a hero of romance, and
expecting unlimited indulgences from my chivalrous
devotion. I can hardly regard her in the light of a rational
creature, so obstinately has she persisted in forming a
fabulous notion of my character and acting on the false
impressions she cherished. But, at last, I think she begins
to know me."*

Emma doesn't wait to see what happens. She just jumps into
the rowboat, unties it from the dock with shaking fingers, and

rows out into the lake. She lets go the oars and drifts. The wind keeps changing direction, swooping down to the lake like a swallow, manipulating the lake's surface into a patchwork, rough then glassy smooth. When Emma rows back in, the beach is empty.

Alone in the cabin, Emma makes herself a sandwich. Peanut butter and jelly. Something her mom would make. Her uncle is next door playing cards with the neighbours. Her aunt is weeding the small garden, oblivious to the bank of clouds building in the sky. Emma doesn't know where Tory's gone. She tells herself she doesn't care, though she's begun to worry about her. Lately, Tory has stopped eating, at least Emma never sees her eat in the cabin. But she seems to be getting fatter anyway. Her breasts look swollen, her cheekbones blunted.

The curtains begin to twist and flail in the wind. The sudden weight of rain does not stop their mad dance. The family portraits perched on the coffee table scatter. Rain pours in through the screens, drenching the books Emma left on the window sill.

"Close the windows," her uncle bellows as he comes running in and the edge of his voice spurs Emma to action. They are all inside now, watching the storm, safely behind glass. Except Tory.

Emma asks where she is, but mid-question catches sight of Tory's white dress in the blur of rain. On the lake side of the cabin. Soaked to the skin, she stands looking up. She does not flinch when the rain turns to hail, batters down on her smooth white face. Tory says nothing as her father drags her inside, holding too tight to her elbow. When he lets go, he leaves fingerprints on her skin. Emma stares at Tory's wet dress, at the dark shadow of pubic hair just visible beneath the jut of her belly.

The uproar passed away in twenty mintures, leaving us all unharmed; except Cathy, who got thoroughly drenched for her obstinacy in refusing to take shelter, and standing bonnetless and shawless to catch as much water as she could with her hair and clothes. She came in and lay down on the settle, all soaked as she was, turning her face to the back, and putting her hands before it.

Emma has trouble sleeping that night with Tory still silent in the bunk below her. The rain has finally stopped but the wind continues to batter the cabin. She listens to the frantic whispering of the poplars, then the boat slamming up against the dock. Someone should have pulled it ashore.

Emma dreams herself back in the rowboat, fishing rod in hand. Tory is skiing nearby, round and round in circles. Not laughing and sunburnt this time, but as blanched and absent as she looked in the rain. Emma casts her line toward Tory. Instead of the satisfying clicks of a gentle reel-in, the line tugs at her. Not a fish, just some weeds perhaps. Then she realizes she is being drawn into the eddy Tory has created. The two of them together, going under.

Emma wakes to a sunrise bright as a perch's belly. She hears the jangle of lures as her uncle fusses with the tackle box on his way out to the boat. Then the strangled sound of Tory retching in the bathroom.

When Emma comes out of the bedroom, Tory is sobbing, Aunt June cradling her like a baby.

"Do we have to tell him?" Tory asks.

"It'll be okay, dear. We'll get through this."

They both become aware of Emma at the same time. "Could you give us some privacy?" Aunt June demands. "We need to be just family right now."

Emma doesn't remind them she is family. She thinks they want to keep her out of it so she doesn't carry back tales to her parents.

Emma knows what's going on anyway, from what she heard through the wall this morning, from what she's guessed. She's just not sure who. She knows Steve doesn't believe in doing it before you're married. When a girl at Emma's school got pregnant, her mom explained everything. She even showed Emma pictures from her nurse's books.

Emma blunders back to her secret clearing, scaring off an indignant prairie chicken and her brood. Emma turns again to *Wuthering Heights*. In this book, women just have babies without sex or pregnancy. Cathy and Isabella. Cathy was just sick for a long time, crazy like Tory in the rain, then her daughter was born out of nowhere.

Emma gets back to the cabin just after her uncle. She doesn't go in. She listens on the porch, through the screen door. Tory whispers and cries. Aunt June clucks. Her uncle says just one word: "Slut."

> *"My young lady is looking sadly worse for her change of condition," I remarked. "Somebody's love comes short in her case, obviously: whose, I may guess; but perhaps, I shouldn't say."*

> *"I should guess it was her own," said Heathcliff. "She degenerates into a mere slut!"*

That night, Emma dreams Brian and her uncle as Heathcliff and Hindley. They are playing poker at the small kitchen table. Tory stands behind her father in her white dress. She's the prize they're gambling for. When Brian carries Tory off, over the threshold, out instead of in, her uncle becomes Heathcliff. He's in the shed with Emma, his rough hands on her breasts. Her nipples rise in spite of herself.

In the morning, Aunt June and Tory prepare to drive into the nearby town. It's Wednesday, the day the doctor is at the clinic there. Aunt June suggests Emma stay at the cabin, but she stubbornly refuses.

"Okay,"Aunt June says. "Come with us. But we have errands to do. You can do the wash at the landromat while you wait for us."

Emma has never done laundry before. She reads the instruc-
tions on the detergent box and separates the clothes into whites
and colours like it says. She has a vague memory of watching her
mom's cleaning lady do this. Then she loads each pile into the
front of a machine, measures in the detergent and sets them going.
This part is not familiar, glass doors at the front of the machine
instead of solid ones on top.

Emma watches the white clothes spin. Somehow, her black
T-shirt has found its way into the load. It whips round, entwined
with a towel, then a sheet, then a pair of Tory's white cotton
underpants. She imagines the whole load coming out grey from
the dye bleeding out of that one little T-shirt, like words blurring
against a page, dissolving in rainwater.

Emma takes the tattered copy of *Wuthering Heights* out of her
beach bag. She recalls the scene where Cathy is horrified that
Linton can find solace in his books even as the world tumbles
down around him: Cathy ill and Isabella gone away with brutal
Heathcliff. She slides the novel down the counter, away from
herself.

A young woman comes in with two garbage bags full of
laundry. Emma guesses a lot of diapers by the smell. She's a few
years older than Tory, her dark hair not as shiny. After she starts
her wash, she notices the book beside Emma.

"Is that yours?" she asks.

Emma surprises herself with a "no." She hasn't finished it yet.

The woman settles into a plastic chair with the book while she
waits for her laundry to come clean.

Jigsaw

For once, there's not a sound coming from next door. Usually I can hear her voice through the wall, even with my TV turned up full. It started the first day I moved in. "You're not listening," she said. "You don't hear me."

I've lived in the next apartment nearly two years now, and I've never seen her. A thin grey-faced man carrying in groceries, but never her. She used to threaten him, but now it's always herself. "What if I killed myself?" she'll ask. "Would you be sorry then?" He never answers back.

I moved to Regina, into this basement suite, when Bill left for good and our house was sold. It's kind of lonely, so I keep the TV on all the time, except when I'm sleeping. I don't even have my cats. They're not allowed here. I had to send them up to my sister and her husband in Saskatoon. Sometimes my sister phones to tell me how they are.

Bill phones too, but mostly to argue about my support payments. It wasn't like that when he first left, before I lost the house in Chamberlain. I'd spend my days in the kitchen baking and stuff. Making it a home he'd want to come back to, like the magazines say. It was a beautiful kitchen, the cupboards all white with yellow handles and the mixing bowls and utensils yellow to match. The window faced west, so I could sit at the table and read in full sun while supper was cooking, the cats purring in the wicker chairs opposite.

By evening though, I'd start to get restless. I'd be sure all day he was coming, then suddenly just as sure he wasn't. I'd find some excuse to go to the store up where the highway cuts through the town, and I'd linger there watching for his truck. There was always an interesting magazine article to browse through. "Playing For Keeps: How to Hold His Interest", or "Win Him Back With Our Ten Day Diet".

I'd have to hide the titles from Gladys, the cashier, or she'd lumber over and stand behind me snickering. Her husband had died. It was the only respectable way to lose a man in that town, and even then someone'd hint the wife had killed him. No one said that about Gladys though. It was her who did most of the hinting.

I could tell she liked having someone to talk to in the evenings, even me. She'd gossip about everyone in town as if it was just between us. How Sally Richards' daughter Sheila had run off to Calgary to be a singer, and her only fifteen. And how the delivery man from Coke, the young fellow with the moustache, had been seen leaving Betty Adams' house awful early in the morning.

She'd always move on to me though. "You should've come to the dance at the Elks' last night Annie," she'd say, pausing to push a grey-blonde curl out of her eyes. "Everyone was asking about you. I told them I see you here. Often." Then she'd smile, but only with her mouth. I'd keep on staring past her out the window.

And sometimes Bill did come. I could see the rusting green cab of his truck down the highway, miles before he got to town. I'd have just enough time to get back to the house and pretend I wasn't waiting.

He wouldn't ring or anything. Just came in as if he still lived there. He'd always been on the road so much, it didn't seem that different anyway. He'd eat the supper I'd made, smoke a cigarette on the porch, then climb into bed beside me.

I'd try to talk to him about things sometimes. If it really was over, or if those brief trips back meant we were together again. He'd say not to push it, not to push him. He never was very good at expressing his feelings. Not from the first. I remember his proposal. My parents kept hinting we should get married, and finally one day he just shrugged and said he guessed we might as well.

I'm sure now he never really meant to come back. I think he just wanted to be sure I still needed him. And of course I did.

I'd never been with any other man. I didn't know how else to live.

After I moved here, listening to the woman next door got to be a bit of a relief from my own troubles. I started piecing her life together, like a jigsaw, from the bits of information I was able to overhear.

I used to love jigsaw puzzles. My favourite was a huge one of a country house in France. It was a white house under a blue, blue sky and the lawn was full of people sipping wine under gay, fringed umbrellas. I did it over and over again, the umbrellas first and the sky last, easiest to hardest.

I'd have to work fast, though, to finish it before Bill got home from a trip, or he'd sweep the whole thing off the table with the cuff of his jacket, to make room for his glass or his plate.

One morning I discovered that she's a student, same as me. "I can't find it. I don't know where I put it," she said, her voice rising almost to hysteria. "I'll fail if I don't hand it in today. I'll fail and you don't care enough to help me." I started school when my support payments came through. I figured I was lucky just to get money from the house, but my lawyer said I should get support too. I couldn't see why he should give me any of his wages if I wasn't his wife anymore, but my lawyer made it sound right.

She reminded me that I'd quit my job to look after him. That I'd spent the last eighteen years cooking and doing his laundry. She said the money would make up for my lost chances, for the career I'd given up.

I still wasn't sure. Waitressing at the truck stop didn't seem like a career.

But she said it didn't matter what I did before. The court would see it her way and give me at least two years of payments. She said I could go to school or something. Retraining she called it.

I wasn't sure I was smart enough for school, but I figured I'd take the money and try it. I'm halfway through my degree now. I think I want to be a social worker. I like to talk, but I can listen too, and I know all about people's problems. I've been reading all the magazines for years. And I got a B+ on my last psychology assignment.

I always stay at school as late as I can on Fridays, putting off spending a weekend in my empty apartment. It was already getting dark when I made my way down the hallway to my door this weekend. But when I got there, I found a card hanging on the doorknob, like one of those "Do Not Disturb" signs, except with the name of a florist printed on it. When I flipped it over, I saw there was a message on the back, but there wasn't enough light out there to read by.

Inside, I switched the lamp on in the living-room and fished in my purse for my glasses. "You weren't in when we came by with your delivery. We left it for you at apartment 8." Apartment 8, their place next door. I thought about finally seeing what she looks like before it occurred to me to wonder who could've sent me flowers.

Then I thought of Bill. Who else would send me flowers? And Saturday would've been our twentieth wedding anniversary. The first year we'd been together, I got all dolled up in lacy pajamas, though I never was the glamorous type. And after that, when I got too fat, I still tried to make it nice with candles and things. It was an effort to push all that out of my mind. "I don't want him now," I told myself. "I'm fine without him. He's never been here and I've never expected him."

There was no one home at number 8, so I concentrated on dinner. Pork chops, mashed potatoes, broccoli, white sauce. I always make a proper dinner. Even back then, everyone in town marveled over what I could do with so little housekeeping money. I have a microwave that my sister and her husband gave me last Christmas, but I don't take any shortcuts. I just use it for heating up when I make too much. I still make too much.

I knock into something every time I turn around in my little kitchen, but it doesn't slow me down anymore. I got supper on the stove fast, then sat down in the living-room and tried to relax. I couldn't help picturing Bill looking around the room. I don't know what he'd think. It's practically empty, except for my chair and my TV. My battered, orange chair. Its arms are all torn up as if the cats got at it, but it's just me tugging at loose threads. I can't seem to stop myself.

I switched off the lamp so I could watch people's legs coming up the walk. I was anxious about the flowers, and still there was no one at number 8. Whenever someone approached, I'd listen for the outside door to slam, then rush to my peephole to see if it was one of them. I'm on a corner, so I have a full view of their door. Of course someone could've come in the back way, so I rang on their doorbell every time a commercial came on, until it got too late.

I spent a lot of the weekend wondering about her. I realized that I could've seen her before at school without knowing it. Maybe she's one of those fresh-faced girls with long, slippery hair, I thought. The ones that wrinkle their noses at each other when I sit next to them in class. I'm glad now that Bill never would agree to have children. I bet my own daughter would've sneered at me just like that.

I try to talk to those girls, but they won't let me. They don't want to hear. They show off sparkly engagement rings to each other. They don't want to know how things can turn out. Everything I say is cut off by their sharp giggles.

I decided that she couldn't be a girl like that. A girl so young and sure wouldn't be with a man as grey and faded. And surely she wouldn't threaten her own life. She must be older, I thought, closer to my age. I hope she's older.

I remember one other time, hearing sounds through the wall that I couldn't identify. Slipping and tearing and jangling. Then I figured it out. She was wrenching clothes off hangers and flinging them down on the floor. "I can't wear any of these things," she said. "They don't fit anymore, nothing fits. Nothing."

It's Sunday night now and finally I see him, fumbling with the lock next door. I wait a few minutes before I go over, so it doesn't look like I've been watching. When I ring, he opens the door with a blank face. He doesn't know who I am and he's forgotten the flowers. Maybe they're dead in their wrapper by now, three days without water.

"Um, there were flowers for me, I think they're here. I mean, they said they left them here." I flutter my florist's card at him.

"Oh," he says. "Oh, yes."

He steps back and looks around the room, and I take the chance to follow. It's just that, one room, a bachelor. The couch is pulled out into a double bed but she's not there, and there's really no sign of her. I can see a few dresses hanging in the open closet, but not enough for somebody else to be still living there.

I feel sick for a minute. What if she's actually done it. Does he look paler than usual? But she can't have. I would've heard something. An ambulance or something. Then it dawns on me, maybe she just left, left this thin, whispery man, this cramped, dingy apartment. Maybe she got away.

He spots the gaily wrapped cone on top of his fridge and hands it over, relieved. I've got the paper half off before I reach my door. I'd pictured roses, though no one's ever sent me any, but it's a bouquet of carnations in bold, false colours.

I have to stop and fuss with my door. I always lock it, even when I'm going down the hall to the laundry. I get in finally, and my fingers tremble as I put the bouquet down on the table and search for the card. Right away I see Bill's scrawl at the bottom. I hurry to put on my glasses so I can read the rest.

"You're cut off, baby. Who's going to pay for those little classes now?"

I sit down on the cracked, vinyl chair and swallow hard. I can see his face, writing that. Feel the edge of his laughter striking me. Then I have to think about it. The last night, the last time he came back before it all fell apart.

It started the same as every other time he came back. The dinner, the cigarette, the silence until we went to bed. Even the lovemaking, he did everything the same every time. But the sameness was comforting to me. I woke up later, drowsy and warm, fooling myself like always that he was back for good.

He was up, standing in the middle of the rag rug I'd made, staring at me. Suddenly he pulled the blanket off me and looked me over with hard, blue eyes. Said he couldn't believe he'd fucked a fat, old woman like me again, after all the girls he'd had on the road. And he was out the door laughing before I could gather the blanket round me, cover myself with it.

Fucked, he said. Fucked, like there was no love at all. Like no one could ever love me with my stretch-marked belly and thighs. Stretch marks and no children to show for them. I bring my fist down on the head of a carnation, and the petals scatter across the table.

I scrape my chair back over the linoleum and look at them, pieces of blue, blue as the French sky in my jigsaw. I must still have it, stored away with other odds and ends in the linen closet, and I want to put it together again.

This time, though, I fancy I'll find myself in it, under an umbrella with a glass of wine in my hand. Me and the woman next door maybe, talking about something we learned in school. This time, I'll finish it, slowly and carefully, the umbrellas first, the sky last, easiest to hardest.

Open Spaces

Beatrice feels very small in the crowded airport. It is as if she shrunk to the size of the people in the tiny cars and farmhouses she saw from the plane as they lifted away from Saskatoon, and she has not yet regained her normal size. She holds tightly to her mother's hand while her father secures a rental car. They are in England now, a very long way from home. She was born here, but she does not remember it, nor the grandparents and aunt who regularly send her Christmas and birthday cards with British stamps.

She celebrated her ninth birthday just before they left home, the first party to which she did not invite boys. Her parents do not often raise their voices, but they argued then. It was absurd, her father said, to plan a party when they were busy packing for such a long trip. Her mother said that this was the very reason for it, a summer is a long time to a child and Bea ought to have a proper chance to say good-bye to her friends.

On the scheduled day, several girls arrived in crisp party dresses and patent leather shoes. They played musical chairs with cushions on the back lawn, ate ice cream and opened presents while Lewis Henry sat on the front steps alone. Lewis and Bea had been friends for as long as either could remember, and he seemed not to believe he had not been invited this year. He sat outside, shoulders round with the injustice of it, until the girls, grass-stained, hair slipping out of ribbons, disappeared one by one into station wagons and sedans. Only then did he slink away, leaving his gift in the mailbox.

His mother must have picked it out — a blank book with a pretty cloth cover that had the words "My Trip" embossed on it in fancy gold letters. Bea carries this gift with her now in a small, white vinyl purse. She grips the purse so tightly, her fingers disappear into its whiteness..

The road is twisty and the car smells too new, like plastic. The English landscape compresses her further as they wind through it. She feels as if she is trapped in the pages of a Beatrix Potter book, everything small and perfect and too close together. Dark green hedges press against the sides of the car. She remembers choosing these books from the children's library, long ago, because she thought she saw her own name on the cover.

Her grandmother, thin and wrinkled, addresses her solemnly as "Beatrice". At home, she told her mother she was grown up enough to be Beatrice, not baby Bea. But in this place, in this unfamiliar accent, so much stronger than her mother's or her father's, the full name does not fit. She disappears in it, as in an over-sized sweater.

She thought she would write in her book about these new relatives, but she does not know what to say. No matter how long she stays here, she does not think she will know them. Her grandmother rarely speaks to her; she seems to think Bea is not very bright. Her grandfather shouts, making her jump each time. He is deaf and cannot hear Bea's thin voice when she tries to answer his questions. Her aunt leans in close when she talks and hugs Bea more often than she likes.

So she writes about the food. She does not like it. Every meal comes encased in pastry, thick and soggy as the English sky. The meats all sound horrid — tongue, liver, kidney. She thinks again of the cows that dotted the prairie. She sits at the kitchen table penciling in painstaking detail a description of each dish, her own tongue pressed firmly against the space left by a front tooth that has fallen out.

At first she at least ate the sweet things her aunt passes around the sitting room for afternoon tea. Apple cake, scones, small fat donuts and shortcake biscuits. But she no longer has an appetite even for these. She eats only toast and weak, milky tea, the colour of the fields she dreams at night. She has heard people back home speak of "wide open spaces". Sometimes she repeats this phrase to herself, lisping the *s*'s slightly, while she drifts to sleep in the soft, creaky spare room bed.

Bea's mother is worried about her, tells her father she is wasting away to nothing. Her narrow, white face is lost in wispy, brown hair. Her summer sprinkle of freckles is already fading.

Bea's aunt joins her at the kitchen table and tells her about another girl's diary, *The Diary of Anne Frank*. She finds a dusty copy of it in the oak bookshelves in the study and reads to Bea. Perhaps you could write your diary like that, dear, she says, address it to a friend. Bea cannot think about her friends; instead, she lies in the big bed and wonders what it would be like never to go outside.

Now Bea is going to Amsterdam. Her parents have decided to make a side trip there before they go home, to see an old school friend of Bea's mother. They say it would be a shame not to go while they are so close. Bea does not want to go. But she does not want to stay in England either, amidst her grandmother's silence, her grandfather's loud voice and her aunt's stifling hugs.

Back on a plane, Bea is afraid this time she will disappear altogether. She imagines herself paper thin, sliding into the pocket of the seat in front of her, between two glossy magazines, or pressed between her diary and Anne's, crammed together now in her vinyl purse. She eyes the sick bag but there is nothing in her stomach. She sucks hard on the barley sugar candies her aunt gave her. Their smooth taste keeps her throat open when she feels she cannot breathe.

Her parents take her along narrow, cramped streets to see Anne Frank's house. They have seen canals, tulips, windmills and wooden shoes. This is different. Bea's father marvels that you cannot see from outside the Annex where the Franks hid. Inside, her mother points out pages of the real diary on display behind glass. Bea cannot imagine all those people living so long in this small space. The blank white walls press against her chest, her stomach. She asks to go back to the hotel.

The next afternoon, while Bea's mother visits with her friend in a café, her father takes her to the Van Gogh museum. Her mother says she is too young to appreciate it, but her father says it will be educational, an opportunity she ought not to miss.

Bea's father takes the audio tour. Headset on, he wanders from painting to painting in careful order. At first, Bea tags close behind, but soon she is darting back and forth across the gallery faster than she has moved in weeks. The tightness in her chest disappears before bright yellow fields and vivid blue skies.

She stops finally and stands for several minutes in front of one particular painting, *Bedroom at Arles*. The emptiness of the room draws her, the sturdy simplicity of the wooden bed frame. It has none of the cushions and doilies and porcelain knick-knacks of her grandparents' house. It is not like the hotel room with twin beds and metal cot covered in thin corduroy blankets. It is plain and practical like her bedroom at home.

Bea's father buys her a postcard miniature of the painting for a souvenir. She slips it carefully into the small, white purse. All the way back to the hotel, she clutches her father's sleeve with one hand, and with the other she swings the purse back and forth by its strap.

At dinner, she does not order toast. She chooses peach melba, a sticky dessert piled high with whipped cream. It is like eating the golden prairie sun. Her mother frets that she will be ill but her father says, why not, at least she's eating again. He boasts about her taste in art, her being able to pick out a famous painting at only nine-years-old.

Bea sits cross-legged on the cot in her nightie staring into the postcard. She knows she will go home and play hide'n'go seek and kick-the-can with Lewis. She has forgotten she does not like boys. In between games, they will sit on the front steps and she will tell him about windmills and wooden shoes and peach melba. She lists them in her book so she will not forget.

A World of Blue

The people who've rented the hall for their wedding reception want an "ethnic" meal, so Sonia's bustling around the kitchen making cabbage rolls and sausage.

Harry can picture the smells wafting out of the kitchen, thick and white like in a comic strip. He sniffs the garlic appreciatively and dunks his mop back into the pail. Sonia will take her supper break soon and he'd like to sneak in and have a taste. He won't, though, he doesn't dare.

Sonia's small and wiry, not fat like you'd expect a cook to be. She's like a sparrow, with her dark eyes and her brown hair soft in a bun. Most of the time she's laughing but if anyone interferes with her food she gets fierce. There'd be trouble if she caught Harry sneaking around the kitchen. For sure she'd stop giving him leftovers.

Sonia's expected to throw everything out after a party but she neatly wraps the leftovers in wax paper and gives them to Harry. She's been a widow for more than ten years, but she hasn't lost the habit of looking after people.

Lots of times the midnight supper is just cold meat, usually ham, and potato salad or coleslaw. But sometimes it's a feast like tonight's. Harry always means to get himself a microwave to reheat things, you can get a small one cheap now. But he hasn't got around to it so he covers Sonia's gifts in foil and warms them in the oven. He'd like to have some of her cooking right off the stove instead of warmed over.

Mostly he eats out of tins. Soup or ravioli on the couch in front of the TV. It seemed glamorous when he was a young bachelor new to the city. In his fifties, now, he's weary of it. He likes to imagine himself with Sonia, eating a proper meal, facing each other across his small kitchen table.

Harry watches game shows if he's home over the supper hour. "Jeopardy" and "Wheel of Fortune". Ordinary guys winning thousands before half an hour's up. Later he chooses one of those live cop shows or "Rescue 911" on cable. Money and heroic deeds. He wonders if that's the kind of man Sonia wants, a hero like in the romance novels she sighs over while she waits for the oven's timer to buzz.

The girl who helps Sonia at the hall is fat — fat and blotchy. Except when she smokes a cigarette, then her face gets thin. Harry can never remember the girl's name.

Pretty soon he sees Sonia and the girl crossing the room to the cubbyhole under the stairs where they eat supper.

"Got time for a break?" Sonia asks.

"Sure, in a minute." He's almost done with the floor, but he wants to stand there with the smells for a bit longer. And he's afraid the girl will make him play cards. Sonia only knows Go Fish. The girl tries to teach her other games but Sonia doesn't catch on. Then Harry plays just to be nice, same as in the old days, long evenings playing Kaiser in the farmhouse with his mother and her sisters.

He's the only one who's expected to stay till the end of the party. Sonia and the girl don't do the serving. Mr. Douglas, the hall manager, gets high school kids to do that. Boys with strange haircuts halfway up their heads and girls with big smiles and blonde, bobbing ponytails.

But Sonia stays anyway, he guesses because she likes to know what the people say about her food. She makes the girl stay too. After the meal, whoever organized the party always asks for a round of applause for the Cook. Sonia comes out in a fresh apron, blushing and dragging the girl behind her.

"Harry," the girl calls in her hoarse voice. "Come and have a game of cards."

"In a minute," he says again. He slides his mop over the last square of tile and stands back to admire the room. The tables are covered with fresh white cloths, each place set with a net bag filled with foil-wrapped sweets, and a blue napkin that has the names of the bride and groom on it in silver. Leonard and Beatrice. The blue and white streamers he strung round the room earlier reflect in the cutlery and now in his freshly-washed floor.

The band has already set up. Harry reckons it's at least a five-piece from the jumble of equipment on the stage. He thinks it would cost a lot to hire a band like that now. "It'll be a fancy crowd tonight," he mutters. "A fancy crowd thinking they're real down home eating Sonia's cabbage rolls."

He used to play in a band himself when he was a kid still living on the farm. Every Saturday night, hair slicked flat to his head, awkward in a suit and a bow-tie, he'd strap on his accordion and get on stage with his Uncle John's band. Uncle John liked the boys to look all shined up for weddings and parties. For barn dances they could wear plaid shirts.

They played at all the little towns nearby but lots of times it was the same crowd. Harry would watch for Rebecca. She was a blonde girl, tall and fine-featured, the kind of girl his mother always said was too thin. She'd dance right in front of the band, whirling around in a full skirt. He wanted to dance with her, to be enveloped in that whirling softness. Especially to "The Blue Skirt Waltz," the words always made him think of her.

Blue were the skies and
Blue were your eyes
Just like that blue skirt you wore . . .

But the boys in the band never got to dance. Besides, he wouldn't have had the courage to ask her.

He left the farm, and the band, right after they played at Rebecca's wedding.

Harry sits down at the nearest table. He picks up a soup spoon and stares at it, twirls it this way and that. In one side, he's even shorter and pudgier than he really is, his face thick and pasty. In the other, he's just a speck, a blur in the grandness of that room. He sees he's smudged the stem of the spoon and polishes it hurriedly on his green work pants.

"Harry," Sonia calls. "Come and have a coffee. It's fresh-made."

"Right away," he shouts back, hoisting himself out of the chair in the direction of his mop and pail. He turns back, looks again at the table, then at the door. He snatches up a bag of sweets and stuffs it into his trouser pocket.

Sonia's smiling at him from her corner. Her hands look so soft and pretty folded in her lap. Harry wants to reach out and put a hand over hers. Or pull the candy out of his pocket and give it to her grandly. Sweets to the sweet. They should be hers. And for once the girl's not paying attention to them, concentrating instead on a game of Solitaire. It's like a moment alone with Sonia.

He's just about to speak when Mr. Douglas, in his booming voice, calls from the kitchen for Sonia. She hurries out.

Harry heard the band clattering into the big room to warm up, but he didn't hear the kitchen door slam behind Mr. Douglas. He's usually so loud.

Mr. Douglas is a big man with wild, dark hair and a beard. He jokes with the women but he never has anything to say to Harry. Not in the whole ten years since he hired him. Harry doesn't like Mr. Douglas, doesn't like the way he treats Sonia. Always flirting with her, but calling her "the help" when he speaks to customers.

Harry takes his tuna sandwich from the little fridge in the corner and chews on it absently. He can hear the rumble of Mr. Douglas's voice from the kitchen now, that low tone he saves just for Sonia. And Sonia responding with a shy giggle that doesn't sound like her. Mr. Douglas's voice booms out again, loud enough for Harry to hear the words: "You keep cooking like that Sonia, and one day I'll marry you." He laughs and Sonia giggles back.

Mr. Douglas looks a lot more like the dashing men on the covers of Sonia's romance novels than he does. This year, Sonia gave Harry a valentine. He knows everyone at the hall got one, but he saved it anyway, placing it carefully inside the cover of a song book he'd kept from his days with the band. He wonders now if Mr. Douglas's card had the same old-fashioned picture of cupid on the front, if Sonia signed it "love" or "yours truly".

"I won," the girl says. "I'm the best."

"Better than who?" Harry snorts. "You're playing solitaire."

The girl looks surprised. "Well, look who's got a tongue finally. You and me'll play a game then. How about Cribbage?" She's already reaching for the board.

"I don't want to play."

The girl's eyebrows arch a little higher.

Harry swallows the last bite of his sandwich and crumples the brown paper bag. He throws it at the metal garbage can in the corner, too hard. It pings off the rim. He sits there, doesn't even tap his foot to the rock and roll number the band runs through first.

Then he hears the opening bars of "The Blue Skirt Waltz" and he has to poke his head out from behind the stairs to watch them.

> *I dream of that night with you*
> *Darling when first we met*
> *We danced in a world of blue*
> *How can my heart forget . . .*

He imagines himself up there in place of the lanky, long-haired keyboard player, and he pictures Rebecca again, her first dance with her new groom.

Instead Harry's looking at Mr. Douglas and Sonia in the doorway of the kitchen, their heads tilted close together. He takes a deep breath, squares his shoulders and strides toward them. The girl follows, a quizzical look on her face.

Harry taps Mr. Douglas purposefully, like he's cutting in. "Sonia, you want to dance?"

Sonia laughs, blushes and holds her arms out to him. The girl is smirking at Mr. Douglas across the room but now Harry doesn't care. He and Sonia are whirling round and round.

> *Blue were the skies and*
> *Blue were your eyes*
> *Just like that blue skirt you wore*
> *Come back, blue lady come back*
> *Don't be blue anymore . . .*

Harry's not much of a dancer, but Sonia lets him lead.

Ghostwriting

Sometimes I think I'm ghostwriting for a ghost. That since Alicia died, she's been trying to speak through me. I know that can't be right, that I can really only be telling my own stories. But since she died, I seem to have twice as many. They get tangled up in each other and catch in my throat before I can get them on paper.

I tried to write a novel once. I didn't actually write any of it down, but I thought about it so hard that I started bumping into my characters in cafés and bars. They'd appear on the edge of a crowd then disappear again just as quickly. I'd see them out of the corner of my eye. Gypsy Louise and her obsessive lover Leo.

Now Alicia flits in and out of my vision like that, a character in my stories. And I can always hear her. Sometimes egging me on when I've already had too much to drink. Other times telling me to go home before I get myself in trouble. Or just whispering over my shoulder at the typewriter.

Other times, I think she's not the words, but the page. She was always giving me blank books to write in. Bulky books with clean, white pages and vivid paintings reproduced on the covers. So the words are mine, but I'm inscribing them on her body. The way she inscribed messages on herself with whatever sharp objects she could find toward the end. Each of my stories is an elaborate tattoo inked on her absent body. My skin is blank. My face blank. White as a sheet.

I always imagined ghosts in grainy black and white, an old movie on late night television. But not Alicia. Gauzy chiffon in deep jewel colours, purple and green. She once told me that purple is the woman colour and green the life colour. Dead, she's still got a bit of each.

She sent black and white postcards when I moved away. Scenes from classic films. Ingrid Bergman in *Gaslight*. Or still lifes. Two martini glasses, one tipped over on its side, and a bottle of vermouth on a silver tray. She said she sometimes felt like that in the hospital, as if she'd been stopped mid-sentence, the words draining out of her.

For a going away gift, she gave me two sturdy tea mugs with fish painted on their sides. Martini glasses would have been more appropriate she said. We drank a lot of tea, but we'd shared more martinis. She was afraid glasses wouldn't travel well. One of the mugs shattered on the journey anyway, I never told her that.

I meant to glue it back together. Crazy Glue softening still visible cracks. I think of Alicia like that now. The scars that veined her body the places where the clay joins again. I worried at the time about which of us was the broken one. I'm still not sure.

We used to sit across from each other in cafés, writing in our journals. Tea or hot chocolate and currant scones. The first time, she was writing her statement to the police. She didn't want to tell me about it, she just wanted me to be there. I was plotting my future somewhere else while she was writing her way to the end of hers.

Alicia didn't want me to leave town, but she was glad for me. From the middle of the prairies to coastal New England. She said if she could, she'd go to the ocean too. Water was always healing for her. We did tarot readings together with a Motherpeace deck and rejoiced if we got the Star or the Moon for an outcome card. The Star signifies opening yourself to the Goddess, asking for help and receiving it. Immersed to her shoulders in a pool, the woman on the card looks at peace with herself. The Moon indicates a swim from darkness into light. This time to her hips in the ocean, the woman dreams herself whole. The first card purple, the second green.

My gift to Alicia was a candelabra of dull metal topped with a crescent moon. She liked to write by candlelight. It was meant for a housewarming gift when the deal on her new house closed, so I didn't give it to her myself. A friend was supposed to give it to her for me on the proper day. I enclosed a note saying that no matter how far away I moved, I'd always be in her tarot house, the tenth position signifying the people who are close to you, who give you strength.

I went to look at the house with her before she decided to buy it. She wanted to know how the place felt to me. She was finally moving away from the neighborhood where it happened, and she wanted to make sure she was moving into a good space. A rambling old house with hardwood floors and a fireplace, all the previous owners seemed to linger there, hanging in the dust the last rays of sunlight illuminated. But Alicia said she didn't mind ghosts as long as they were good ones. We agreed these ones were.

I guess she wasn't in the house much more than a month before she checked herself into the hospital. My friend never gave her the candelabra. He sent it back to me after she died, the note still sealed. It felt odd to tear open the envelope and read my own message. Now I write by candlelight, and sometimes feel her hovering just outside the flickering circle.

When I left for the east coast, she said she'd come visit. We'd take a ferry over to Nantucket or Martha's Vineyard. A sea-side holiday. Then there was the hospital, but she still thought she'd make it. She figured her psychiatrist would give her a pass. In the end I went by myself.

I was waiting for the Nantucket ferry at Hyannisport when I found out. I called from a phone booth for my messages, staring into sea blue as the prairie sky. *Alicia's done it. She's on life support but she won't wake up. Don't come home, not yet.* In a small bed and breakfast I waited for news. I could still feel her and thought then that meant she was alive. I sat on the beach, sifting small piles of sand from one hand to the other, as if I could take back time.

I watched obsessively for the ferry to arrive and leave again. I've always believed in circles. That if you can complete one, write yourself back to the beginning, the hurt won't have happened. The scar heals over. When I got word she was really gone, I took the next ferry out.

The water travelled with me. According to the Airport bus driver, it had been raining across the prairies since the day Alicia died. "Beautiful till Friday, pissing rain ever since." It broke after the memorial service, but by then I was gone again.

I tried to piece Alicia together from the bits that I'd saved. Her postcards, the mug. I was afraid I would lose her. Now I know I couldn't if I wanted to. A phantom limb, the ache of absence.

Once when I was at a low point, she wrote me: "If anyone bothers you about your drinking, just tell them you do it to make other people more interesting." I drink more than I did then. I choose bars where I know no one so I don't have to explain. Sometimes I drink to drown out her words, to wash away her stories, make room for my own. But she clings like smoke to my clothes and hair.

I have to go back to the water to recover myself. Repossess myself. Back to that Nantucket beach where I watched the lights of the ferry disappear as it pulled away from the harbour in the dark. I stand at the water's edge in sunlight and toast her. One last martini. A bottle of gin and a bottle of vermouth dancing in the waves.

Moving Away

She is connected to her lover by a ribbon of highway.

Leaving that morning in his Volkswagen van, she pictured it rolling out behind them, like a measuring tape marking the miles. When he'd first heard she'd got the job and he offered to help her move, she didn't think they could fit everything in his van. After they finished, it was only half full.

They smiled at each other over coffee-stained menus in truck stops, peered earnestly at the price tags of identical weavings hawked in every town as originals. She almost bought one, to remember the trip by, but then she wasn't sure she'd want to remember it once he'd gone back without her.

They pulled up to her new apartment around supper time and unloaded her stuff right away. It didn't take long. In spite of her efforts the apartment looked as forlorn as the van had.

For dinner, she set out two plates of scrambled eggs on an overturned packing box, and he surprised her with a bottle of red wine he pulled from his duffel bag. "It ought to be white with eggs," she teased.

She started work the next morning. He lay back on the mattress watching her dress, arms folded behind his head. He laughed at her struggling into a suit, he'd never seen her wear one before. But there was an edge to his laughter.

When she got home at five, she could see he'd been busy. He'd hung the blinds and tacked up her few posters, pictures of Billie Holliday and Bessie Smith. He'd even found legs for her bed.

"I could tell you didn't like sleeping so close to the floor." He grinned. "I thought I'd leave the hardwood to the spiders."

"Where'd you get them?"

"At that hardware store, across the street."

She'd been there herself on her way home, looking for hangers. It was dim and dusty inside, full of bewildering things that didn't seem to belong together. She didn't know how he'd managed to find bed legs there.

"I'm not an altogether utilitarian guy though," he continued. "I got you something else, from the antique store." He handed her a package, awkwardly wrapped in tissue paper.

It was a silver locket, slightly tarnished, but beautiful still.

"I'll send you a picture to put in it."

She bit her lip.

"Hey, it's not a substitute," he said. "We'll still see each other. It's only a six-hour drive."

Riding the bus back to see him, she stares out the window and slides the locket back and forth on its chain until the links are warm against her neck.

After the first few hours, she begins to fancy the highway disappearing behind her. Their hometown becoming an island while they're together. No roads in, no roads out.

She knows he will be at the depot offering a casual kiss as if he doesn't miss her. She can see him from the window when the bus pulls into the terminal, shifting from foot to foot betraying his impatience.

Between visits, his phone calls are rare, like unexpected pockets of water in a dry river bed. He never seems able to answer her questions. It's as if he doesn't see their old friends anymore. One night he tells her he got a new job at a music store across town from where they used to live. The name of the store doesn't even sound familiar to her.

She toys with the cord while they speak, getting her hair caught in its twisted kinks. Once she had to cut out a piece of hair after she hung up. She thought about sending it to him, a lock of her hair, though it's she who wears the empty locket. She imagines he'd keep it in his wallet next to the photograph of his mother and sister, next to the yellowed newspaper clipping of his father's obituary.

When winter comes, he says there is no time for visits. He has weekends off, but he's too tired to make the trip. Then his calls stop.

She pictures white snakes of snow writhing across the highway, tangling with the phone lines, crackling along the wires. She doesn't call him. She's afraid of an unfamiliar voice on the other end, a woman's voice saying he's out, can she take a message. Or someone telling her he's moved away, disappeared altogether.

She takes to sprawling on her narrow bed and tracing the line on the map. She knows each gentle curve, each bordering lake and slough. She memorizes the name of each town along the way.

Gradually she moves beyond these boundaries. She follows the side roads that jut off at odd angles. She wonders what really happens when the map changes colour, if her eyes would catch the transition from a car window. Then one night she dreams herself outside the map. She sees the world a ball of twine, herself holding the end.